THE HAUNTED BOOKSHELF

he telling or reading of ghost stories during long, dark, and cold Christmas nights is a yuletide ritual dating back to at least the eighteenth century, and was once as much a part of Christmas tradition as decorating fir trees, feasting on goose, and the singing of carols. During the Victorian era many magazines printed ghost stories specifically for the Christmas season. These "winter tales" didn't necessarily explore Christmas themes. Rather, they were offered as an eerie pleasure to be enjoyed on Christmas Eve with the family, adding a supernatural shiver to the seasonal chill.

The tradition remained strong in the British Isles (and her colonies) throughout much of the twentieth century, though in recent years it has been on the wane. Certainly, few people in Canada or the United States seem to know about it any longer. This series of small books seeks to rectify this, to revive a charming custom for the long, dark nights we all know so well here at Christmastime.

THE
HAUNTED BOOKSHELF

THE MORGAN TRUST

THE MORGAN TRUST

R. BRIDGEMAN

A GHOST STORY FOR CHRISTMAS

DESIGNED & DECORATED BY SETH

BIBLIOASIS

ddly enough, it was a small handbook entitled *Not the Highways* that set Selby Pyle on the track of the strange village in the mountains.

He bought the slim volume at the station kiosk because there happened to be a picture of Snowdon on the cover, and he had for some time been toying with the idea of spending a holiday in Wales.

He riffled idly through its pages, noting in passing that it had been written—not very well written—by one John Kilby; as he read, the train rattled him along the way to Guildford where there had been rumours of a cottage with strange noises.

For Selby Pyle, middle-aged gentleman of leisure and assured income, had an unusual hobby. He liked to call himself an "Amateur Psychic Investigator." And when his contemporaries asked, "Why?" he would go into details, explaining that he used the word "Amateur" to denote that he worked without payment, and not because he was lacking in knowledge or experience of his subject.

But if they asked, "Why such a strange hobby?" he would become evasive. "Because it's out of the ordinary," was his usual lame excuse. Only in his more sanguine moments would he admit even to himself the real motive behind his pursuit.

And if they still persisted in their amazement that a portly and immaculately-clad gentleman with cherubic blue eyes, a shapeless blob of a nose which offered only the most precarious of resting-places for rimless spectacles, a soft baby-tight mouth and a series of flabby chins should adopt such a way of spending time and money, then Selby, squirming a little and rubbing his thin flaxen hair with stubby white fingers, would be driven to confess openly certain of his innermost secrets.

He would tell how, despite the fact he was a religious man, he had failed to find solace in the teachings of the Church, and that he had an overwhelming dread of being snuffed out like an ephemeral candle when his time came. He was searching, he would tell them, for proof positive of life in the hereafter. He kept notes and pictures in voluminous folders. On the wall of his study was a large-scale map with the sites of past investigations marked with red dots. He had a supply of small blue flags which were to be used if ever his search proved fruitful. But although the map was a measle-rash of red spots, it was devoid of blue flags.

Every rumour that came to his ears he traced hopefully to its source. So when he read the few lines in his morning paper about the strange happenings at Guildford, he boarded the first train.

London melted away, fields and farms slipped by, and Selby flicked through his booklet, sighed a little and stopped just by chance at the page that contained the description of Cwmbach. "This village," Mr. Kilby informed him through the medium of the pages, "is one of the most isolated that I encountered. Situated in a hollow in the shadow of Crib Goch it is steeped in the past. There is an excellent hostelry—the Bryn Mawr—and I can heartily recommend it as a centre for the enthusiastic fisherman. The roads are in poor condition; the air is mild, being shielded from the northerly winds; the people are friendly, and there is a fund of local superstition and tales of hauntings to delight even the most hardened of travellers."

Selby, himself a writer, wriggled a little at the rather formal and Borrowesque turn of phraseology. But all the same his interest quickened and his psychic nose quivered at the mention of "tales of hauntings." He took out his notebook, made a note of the author's name, and discovered that the publisher of the booklet was a friend of his, who had published certain of his writings.

The Guildford investigation having proved, as he had feared, to be fruitless—a matter of faulty plumbing—Selby wasted no further time: he telephoned the publisher from a kiosk in the High Street. Armed with Mr. Kilby's address he returned to London, dined, and took a taxi to the home of John Kilby, M.A.

The author of *Not the Highways* was angular and elderly, had a domed forehead and watery eyes. He listened to Selby's request for further information about Cwmbach with a certain air of suspicion.

"I take it you are engaged on a similar work?" he commented heavily. Selby went to great pains to protest his innocence of such a thing, whereupon the other unbent enough to produce a file of notes which he explained had been the basis of the book in question.

"It must be three years since I wrote the book," he offered. "Cwmbach," he toyed with the name. "I remember a little. But so far as the—er—supernatural aspect is concerned, I know no more than I wrote. If I had," he pointed out, "then I should have put it in. After all, there is little enough one can write about a place of that size.

"Cwmbach," he said thoughtfully to the ceiling. "Grey stone cottages, a stream that runs down the main street, and some grand views of the valley. But the name brings back something else . . . Now what was it?"

He sat for a while, staring at his notes; Selby waited with some impatience. So far as he was concerned, if Mr. Kilby had nothing more to add about the hauntings, then the interview could well be terminated.

"Morgan," Kilby said into the silence, "—that was the name, Ifor Morgan. There was a picture of him in the pub, and when I asked about it they told me the story."

He stroked his chin, smiling a little. "Not that it can be of any use to you; indeed, it was of no use to me. But interesting, from a psychological point of view, for all that. Ifor Morgan, it seemed, was something of a rascal in his day. Many years ago he set up a kind of a Trust Fund, getting most of the local people to subscribe to it, the idea being that he would build a new village for them; modern houses, you know, bring in power and water on tap. It was going to be built in a green valley, just below Cwmbach, and by all accounts it was going to be a proper Shangri-La.

"But of course, like all plans of that sort, it fell flat. He did start the building, but without previous consultation with the local authority. In the course of time they came down on him like a ton of bricks. A stupid man more than a knave, perhaps; a visionary—a dreamer. There have been many such: their follies litter the country-side. But Morgan took it very badly . . ."

"I take it he is dead?" Selby asked with quickening interest.

"Good Lord, yes. This happened years ago. But the people of Cwmbach talk about it as if it were only yesterday. Three years ago, when I stayed at the Bryn Mawr, there were still some alive who had actually subscribed to the fund, their life savings had gone down the drain. But the strange thing about that—"

"Yes?" Selby encouraged.

"They seemed to bear no animosity. Rather, his memory had been kept alive with affection, almost reverence. Think of it; he'd done them out of thousands, for most of the village had subscribed, and all there is to show for it—and I went to see for myself— is a pathetic collection of grass-covered foundations and partly-built walls.

"There's no accounting for people," he mused. "They forget the money they lost, remembering only that he did try to make things better for them. They were very proud, jealously proud, of Ifor Morgan."

Selby said: "The tales of hauntings, you don't connect them with this unfinished village?"

"Llannef it was to be called," Kilby told him. "I made a note of the name, intending to look up its meaning—I have an interest in Welsh place-names. No, Mr. Pyle, it was merely an idle word dropped by the landlord of the Bryn Mawr that led me to comment about it in my book. Now what was it he said?" He clicked his fingers. "Of course. I asked if there were any local stories—the kind of thing I could put in my book, you know? He said that there are ghosts in any village worth its salt. Perhaps he was trying to be clever. Anyway,

I enlarged upon it, and put it in for what it was worth."

Selby left him then and returned to his own flat, wondering if it would be wasted effort if he were to journey to the mountains in search of the village. And it was only because he'd already decided to go to Wales anyway that he made up his mind to include Cwmbach in his itinerary.

He went by car, starting off early the next morning, striking due north, and spending the night at Chester. The following morning saw him driving through the sunshine of the coast road, crossing the Conway bridge, and swinging through the coastal resorts. At Bangor he turned inland, his map taking him readily enough as far as Bethesda. From there onwards he found it more satisfactory to rely upon local directions and reached Cwmbach in time for lunch.

It was much as he had imagined. The mountains, brown and green with outcroppings of grey granite, almost encircled the village. Cwmbach was typically Welsh, with the small, low-roofed cottages clustered about the steep slate roof and tall chimneys of the inn. A bracken-brown stream bubbled merrily at one side of the main street.

White-aproned women and cloth-capped men smiled at him as he coasted past; children broke off their play to wave. Selby felt a pleasure in their welcome; the mountains behind came down like a curtain, cutting off the world of finance and worry, hydrogen bombs and guided missiles. He swung the car on to the cobbled forecourt of the Bryn Mawr.

He went through an archway, and the landlord, stocky and chestnut-faced, bare-armed and wearing a blue waistcoat with gilt buttons, made quite a thing of shaking his hand.

The bar was a cheerful place, low-timbered and aglow with polished jugs and tankards. A heavy-framed picture on one wall dominated the room, and Selby went to look at it.

It was the portrait of Ifor Morgan of which Kilby had spoken, for the name was written below in a flowing oldfashioned script. The landlord came by his side, asking in a soft lilt if "The gentleman would be staying overnight, or perhaps for longer?"

"A day or two," Selby told him; then, tapping the picture, "A fine-looking man."

"Our Mr. Morgan?" The voice was even softer, and there was certainly reverence. "Indeed, a very fine man."

And as Selby turned to look at the landlord, a phrase came to his mind, brought there by the expression on the brown, wrinkled face: "I will lift up mine eyes . . ."

Ifor Morgan had the face of a patriarch, a deep-eyed, wide-set face that might have come from the Old Testament. He had the eyes of a dreamer, placid and fathomless, but the high forehead of a thinker. His hair was white and luxuriant, falling in uncombed sweeps and folds to frame the broad cheeks and gently-smiling lips.

"I have heard the story of Llannef," Selby said tentatively.

And the other replied, "Have you indeed, sir?" in a tone lacking surprise, as if it were the most natural thing in the world for a stranger to know the story.

After lunch, Selby took his coffee to a small iron table in the forecourt, a placid, very ordinary man in flannels and blue blazer, his spectacles aslant on his face, relaxing happily, the world he had left far away behind the tall cloud-wrapped mountains.

Children played in the sun, laughing and shouting, their voices clear and shrill. Their clothes were bright and clean, new-looking almost, and he remarked on this when the landlord came blinking into the sun.

"All in their best today," he explained to Selby, "and a holiday from school. A celebration it is for everybody to mark the passing of old Gwan Hughes."

Selby wondered idly who Gwan Hughes could have been that the anniversary of her death should be marked by a holiday. He put his thoughts into words, and the landlord looked mildly surprised.

"Early this morning, at dawn, it was, when she breathed her last; ailing for some time, and very old ..."

And Selby, sipping his coffee, with

the children's happy voices about him, thought how pleasant it was that death should be celebrated with laughter and a holiday instead of wreaths and mourning. It seemed so right. For a moment, the constant fear of his own death faded, and he could almost believe that here in Cwmbach he might find that which he had sought throughout the years.

Later, in the peace of his room, when he came to analyse his thoughts, he found it was because these people assumed death to be something that called for rejoicing that his own fears melted. For why should they be so happy, he reasoned, unless it was because they knew death to be something more than just the going out of a light?

After tea—an affair of freshly baked cake and hot buns dripping with butter—Selby tried to bring the conversation round to the story of Ifor Morgan and his village, but the landlord was politely evasive. But not because there was nothing to say about the man and the village that was never completed; Selby got the impression that he was reticent about discussing the matter simply because a "foreigner" wouldn't understand.

The children were still playing in the street, and· Selby watched them for a while, enjoying their holiday from school. From the school, his thoughts drifted to churches and he searched the surrounding rooftops for the spire or steeple that would show its locality. But the village was flat, only the low slate roofs and the mountain slopes.

When the landlord came out, wiping his hands on a blue-edged towel, Selby asked him about a church or a chapel in Cwmbach, and the other smiled, shaking his head. The nearest chapel was beyond the mountains—at Bethesda, no less.

Then Selby got to thinking about the old lady who had just died. "They will have to take her to Bethesda?" he wanted to know.

The landlord smiled again, almost pityingly, and changed the subject to salmon fishing, leaving Selby feeling that in some indefinable way he had been gently rebuffed.

With some idea of exploring the countryside, he went to the car, passed a rag over the windscreen and checked the petrol. The landlord watched the preparations with a slightly worried air.

"A run is it?" he asked. "Perhaps as far back as Bethesda?"

Selby shook his head. "I was thinking of following this road up into the mountains. There should be some excellent views from higher up."

"I wouldn't advise it," the other said carefully. "The roads are bad, and one must be very careful. Night comes down quickly and there is a chance that you might lose yourself. And that, in the mountains, is a very bad thing."

Selby levered himself behind the wheel and adjusted his glasses. He felt a little put out, even annoyed, at the insinuation that he was incapable of looking after himself.

"I'll risk it," he said briefly, and started the car.

The other shouted something above the roar of the engine, and moving down the slope, Selby cupped his ear to catch the words.

"Look out—the fork—keep—to—left—mind you—right . . ."

He waved in acknowledgment of the scattered instructions, smiled a little to himself at the thought of the landlord's concern and swung out into the road.

The cottages fell behind, and the mountains crowded in for a while, then swept away again so that the valley spread itself out far below, a thing of brown and green squares, with the occasional glint and glitter of meandering streams. He stopped to admire the view, leaning out of the window, letting the salt-heavy breeze stir his hair, the tang of the sea on his lips. Life felt very good; there was a peace out here, between the sky and the valley, that he hadn't felt before.

He lay back against the soft upholstery, letting the calm engulf him, then dozed off, nodding gently, fat white fingers laced above the mound of his waist.

So Mr. Pyle slept, suspended between heaven and earth, with the seagulls crying high above, and only the peace of the mountain slopes to hear their calling.

When he awoke, refreshed, the sun was pulling itself down behind the highest peaks; the breeze had freshened and was cooler; dusk was slipping silently about him. The gulls had ceased their clamour, and the very earth seemed to hold its breath.

He started the car, debating for a moment whether or not to retrace his steps, but the lure of the winding road ahead was too strong; he set the bonnet into the cleft of the mountains.

After a while he came to where the road forked, three ways offering invitations, and he tried to remember the instructions flung after him by the anxious landlord. Had he to keep to the right or the left? But what matter when there would be time to explore each in their turn? Tonight it would be the road to the left, for that led up into the mountains, with the trees overhanging, and bushes and gorse thick on its verges.

The sun vanished and night came down like a black cloak. The world was

very still, the air sharp and clear. Breasting a slope where the rocky walls widened, he came on the scattered lights of a village in a hollow. He stopped then, drawing the car well into the side of the road and unfolding his road map in the dim glow of the small roof light.

He managed to trace his path as far as Cwmbach itself, but then the road developed into series of dotted lines. He found the spot where he had slept overlooking the valley, and came upon a small village ahead. He strained over the name, holding the map to catch the light. Pengwyn it was called.

While he pored over the map, he caught sight of a movement, a flicker of movement in the driving mirror above his head. Someone was coming along the road behind, a nebulous white shape that resolved itself into the figure of a woman, dressed in a pale-coloured frock and with a white shawl draped loosely over her head.

She walked with purpose, almost impatiently, with long, firm strides, her face to the village ahead, but turning to look at him as she passed the car, half-raising her arm in a gesture. She smiled into his eyes, the happy smile of a woman who smiled for the very pleasure of life; then she was ahead, a tall shadow in the lights of the car, vanishing into the blackness of the night.

Selby felt his heart warm to her gesture and smile. A woman who had passed, a stranger who had found time to offer her happiness. It was a woman going home, to a house that waited, with a husband and children to welcome her. He felt suddenly very envious of her happiness.

Her face was still bright in his mind when he started the car and slipped down the road, his headlamps cutting clear swathes of golden light. He found himself searching the night for her slim figure, with some idea at the back of his mind of offering a lift. But the houses were around him sooner than he had imagined, and then for a brief moment he saw her, her hand on a gate, sharply outlined in the harsh glare of his lights.

He turned to look back over his shoulder, seeing how the cottage door was open and waiting to receive her, how a dark shadow in the golden oblong held out its arms to welcome. He felt absurdly pleased that he had seen the end of her journey.

He drove slowly through the comforting lights of cottages and houses, stopping finally in the friendly glow of the hotel. The bar was full, a place of noise and laughter. Selby sat in a corner, content to look on and, looking on, to become at one with the place. He felt tired, and the heavy warmth gave a dreamlike quality to the small room and friendly faces.

The landlord was a smiling grey-haired man whose features melted and blurred and he hovered with tray and glasses, speaking of the weather and the crops, of how things were in the valley.

"You have rooms?" Selby asked impulsively.

"But of course . . ." He seemed surprised at the question.

"Tomorrow, then," Selby told him. "I will come back tomorrow; my things are at a hotel in Cwmbach."

"Perhaps it would be better if you were to stay," the landlord offered gently. "There may be no room tomorrow . . ."

He hesitated, then, but borrowed night-clothes offered little attraction. Also, the landlord of the Bryn Mawr deserved consideration. It was only right and fair that he return, at least for the night. But afterwards—he was then prepared to spend the rest of his holiday in Pengwyn.

Mindful of the lateness of the hour, he rose and went out into the darkness. The landlord followed, standing by while he climbed behind the wheel. Then he said something which, at the time, held little sense.

"People don't usually go away again," said he, shaking his head. "There is something here that I don't understand."

"I'll be back," Selby told him sleepily, and drove away into the night.

At the top of the hill he stopped the car and turned to look back, refreshing his memory of the place. It lay there, a toy village in the dark cupped hand of the night. And as he watched, the lights winked out, one by one, until only a pool of darkness remained.

The people of Pengwyn, it seemed, had gone to bed.

Back at the Bryn Mawr, the landlord seemed pleased to see him. His eyes asked a question while his hands were busy with tankards.

"I made it as far as Pengwyn," Selby told him. "A pleasant little place, too; I think I'll move along there tomorrow." He yawned; it was getting late; the old clock above the counter was pointing to eleven.

"Just as you say, sir." The landlord was politely disappointed. A burst of laughter came from the next room, and Selby looked pointedly at the clock. "Your patrons keep late hours," said he, "later than the people of Pengwyn."

"A special day, today," the other explained. "It is the sons of Gwan Hughes who drink to their mother's passing. It would be a pleasant gesture on your part if you were to join them. As for the listening laws ..." He smiled apologetically. "On such a day one turns a blind eye."

Selby went into the other room, noting in passing that a garland of flowers had been draped across the portrait of Ifor Morgan. It was like Christmas in July, but roses and lavender instead of holly.

They greeted him, three brown-faced, happy men, smiling and breaking off their singing to offer him a glass. "For you to drink to our mother," they told him, "for she has left for the other place."

There were others of the village too, men and women alike, all dressed in obvious Sunday finery, all smiling, all openly taking pleasure in the death of Gwan Hughes.

The sons were loquacious in drink, back-slapping and merry.

"And how old would your mother be?" Selby asked, to make conversation.

They discussed the matter earnestly amongst themselves, apparently never having given the matter much thought.

"Seventy-five," the tallest of the three hazarded.

"Not a day under eighty," the one next to him contradicted. "For you will remember she was putting money into the Trust right from the start . . ."

Selby felt a quickening of interest. "The Trust?" he queried, but his words were lost in the good-natured argument that ringed the old lady's age. Comparative ages were being bandied: "Sixteen years since Trevor here paid his first . . ." "Twenty it'll be since I started, and that makes her all of eighty-six . . ."

Then a photograph, a thing of dog-ears and cracks, brown and faded, was produced from a bulky wallet, and Selby was invited to give his opinion. "Taken some years ago, you will understand," he was told, "but you can see that she was a fine woman indeed."

And as he stared at the placid, smiling face he knew that he had seen it before. But not quite like that. Iron away the wrinkles from mouth and eyes, drape a white shawl over the hair . . .

"I have seen this woman before," he told them. "I have seen her this very evening. It was on the road to Pengwyn . . ."

And then a silence fell, with all the faces turned to his. They were puzzled and surprised. But the amazing thing was, he soon discovered, that they were not questioning the fact that he had seen their dead mother, but only that he had seen her on the way to Pengwyn.

The landlord, at his shoulder, asked gently, "Tell us how you got to this village . . . Pengwyn, you call it."

Selby told them, explaining how he had

first fallen asleep, and then driven on until he reached the place where the road forked into three . . . And when he described this, they looked at each other, nodding wisely and significantly.

"And so you took the left-hand road, the old mountain road," the landlord said, offering it as a statement rather than a question.

Selby agreed that he had taken the left-hand road. "Pengwyn," the other explained simply, "lies to the right. It is a mining village, a place of slag heaps and tall chimneys. A place of coal-dust and filth."

His voice was singing, his eyes aglow.

"You took the road to Morgan's village," said he, "to Llannef. And you saw Gwan Hughes on her way home . . ."

SELBY PYLE LIVES in Cwmbach now; he has lived there for upwards of two years.

Sooner or later, he believes that he will be approached to make his contribution to the Morgan Trust, and then he too will be on the list. So that when his time comes, the years will fall from his shoulders, and he in his turn will trace Gwan Hughes's steps along the road that leads to Llannef.

He has been, of course, to the fork in the road, and has seen for himself how it divides into two, with one leading to Pengwyn and the other to two mountain farms.

But there is a third road, an overgrown memory of a road that was hardly ever made, and it leads up into the mountains. It is only the faintest of tracks, and Selby has followed it, coming to the crown of the hill, there to look down on the desolation of coarse grass and ivy-covered rubble which is all that remains of Ifor Morgan's village.

Like all the people of Cwmbach, he knows that sometimes the village is there—a place of lights and happiness—with a road that leads to it, an inviting, smooth highway. He knows, too, that once he has paid his deposit, he will be assured of a house in that village, and that one night the lights will shine out their welcome to him, as they did once before. But the next time he goes into the valley, it will be to stay.

And although he has finally completed his search for proof of life in the hereafter, he still feels regret that there should be a coldly impersonal thing as paying a deposit and putting one's name down for a house.

He wonders, too, if there are likely to be mansions available, as well as cottages. But then, Selby Pyle, like most of us, is something of a snob at heart.

ichard Bridgeman (Leslie Purnell Davies) was a British novelist whose works typically combine elements of horror, science fiction and mystery. He also wrote many short stories under several pseudonyms.

eth's comics and drawings have appeared in the *New York Times*, the *New Yorker*, the *Globe and Mail*, and countless other publications.

His latest graphic novel, *Clyde Fans*, won the prestigious Festival d'Angoulême's Prix Spécial du Jury.

He lives in Guelph, Ontario, with his wife, Tania, in an old house he has named "Inkwell's End."

Library and Archives Canada Cataloguing in Publication

Title: The Morgan trust : a ghost story for Christmas /
R. Bridgeman ; designed & decorated by Seth.
Names: Bridgeman, R. (Richard), 1914- author. |
Seth, 1962- illustrator.
Description: Series statement: Christmas ghost stories
Identifiers: Canadiana 20200279130 |
ISBN 9781771963725 (softcover)
Classification: LCC PR6054.A76822 M67 2020 |
DDC 823/.914—dc23

Readied for the press by Daniel Wells
Illustrated and designed by Seth
Copy-edited by Theo Hummer
Typeset by Tania Craan

PRINTED AND BOUND IN CANADA